This book belongs to

Princess Aidaly Yanirel
Trujillo

The Royal Disney Princess Club

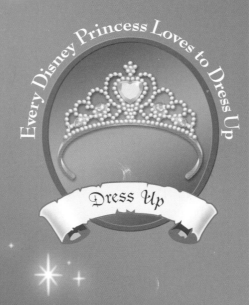

Every Disney Princess Loves to Dress Up

Dress Up

Story adaptation by Annie Auerbach. Crafts and activities by Kris Hirschmann.

Photography by White Light Incorporated, Bethel, CT

Design by Mark A. Neston Design

Published by Scholastic Inc., 90 Old Sherman Turnpike, Danbury, CT 06816.

For information regarding permission, write to: Disney Licensed Publishing, 114 Fifth Ave., New York, NY 10011.

ISBN-13: 978-0-545-08425-3   ISBN-10: 0-545-08425-3
U.K. ISBN-13: 978-0-545-08551-9   U.K. ISBN-10: 0-545-08551-9

Printed in Singapore

First printing, August 2008

Disney PRINCESS

Jasmine

A Storybook with Crafts & Activities

SCHOLASTIC INC.

New York   Toronto   London   Auckland   Sydney
Mexico City   New Delhi   Hong Kong   Buenos Aires

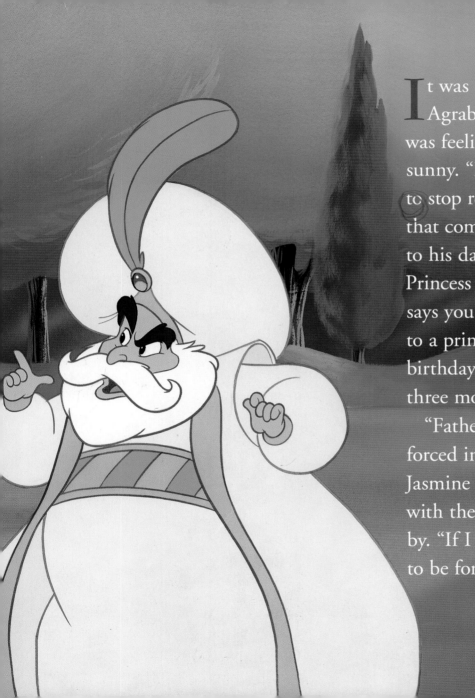

It was a bright day in Agrabah, but the Sultan was feeling anything but sunny. "Dearest, you've got to stop rejecting every suitor that comes to call," he said to his daughter, the lovely Princess Jasmine. "The law says you must be married to a prince by your next birthday. You've only got three more days!"

"Father, I hate being forced into this," Princess Jasmine said, frustrated with the laws she had to live by. "If I do marry, I want it to be for love," she insisted.

Although Jasmine loved dressing up and having beautiful things, she often felt trapped. She longed to leave her royal life behind and see what experiences lay beyond the palace.

So one night, dressed as a villager, Jasmine secretly climbed the palace walls and escaped into the darkness. She soon found herself in the busy marketplace. Her eyes widened with wonder as she took in all the new and exciting sights!

Jasmine spotted a little boy looking at some apples nearby. "Oh, you must be hungry," she said, grabbing an apple from a cart for him.

"No one steals from my cart!" yelled the apple seller, angrily grabbing Jasmine's wrist.

But because she had never had to pay for anything, the princess didn't understand what she had done wrong.

Just in time, a stranger
came to Jasmine's rescue.
"Thank you, kind sir,"
the young man said to
the angry seller. "I'm
so glad you found her.
She is my sister. She's a
little crazy."

Jasmine was puzzled
but played along. The plan
seemed to be working—
until the stranger's small
monkey bowed good-bye, and
more stolen apples fell out of
his waistcoat!

"Come back here, you little
thieves!" the angry fruit seller
shouted, but the three quickly
ran away.

They made their way through the marketplace and ended up on a rooftop. "Is this where you live?" asked Jasmine.

"Yep. Just me and Abu," her new acquaintance said, gesturing to his monkey. "We come and go as we please."

"Fabulous," said Jasmine, envious of his freedom.

Meanwhile, the young man looked wistfully at the palace in the distance.

"Sometimes I just feel so trapped," they said at the same time. The two looked at each other, surprised they felt the same way.

All of a sudden a group of guards burst in.

The young man looked at Jasmine and asked, "Do you trust me?"

Jasmine couldn't deny the connection she felt with this stranger. "Yes," she replied.

"Then jump!" he said, grabbing her hand. The two jumped and landed safely—only to run into more guards.

"It's the dungeon for you, boy!" said Rasoul, the head guard.

Jasmine had to think quickly. It was time to stop playing dress up, pretending she was someone else. "Unhand him. By order of the princess," she commanded, removing her hood.

The guard instantly recognized Princess Jasmine but didn't release the young man. "My orders come from Jafar," said Rasoul. "You'll have to take it up with him."

"Believe me, I will," said Jasmine angrily, while the guards dragged the young stranger away.

Jafar was the royal adviser to the Sultan. Besides being conniving and downright evil, his control over Jasmine's father made the princess despise Jafar.

As soon as Jasmine returned to the palace, she confronted Jafar. But the evil man lied, telling the princess that the young man had already been executed.

"How could you?" Jasmine cried. Heartbroken, the princess ran from the room.

Several days later, there was a grand parade in Agrabah to announce the arrival of Prince Ali Ababwa. Hundreds marched toward the palace—men threw swords in the air and women danced with scarves. There were balloons and banners, peacocks and monkeys, even solid gold camels!

On top of a huge elephant sat Prince Ali, all dressed up and tossing gold coins into the crowd. He was making his way to the palace to woo the princess.

Jasmine watched from her balcony as Prince Ali approached, and she was disgusted by the whole spectacle.

The Sultan, however, welcomed Prince Ali into the palace.

"Just let me meet her," Prince Ali said smugly. "I will win your daughter."

"How dare you!" exclaimed Jasmine, who had been listening to Prince Ali boasting. "Standing around deciding *my* future? I am not a prize to be won!" she said, before storming out of the room.

Determined to make things right with the princess, Ali went to her balcony that evening to apologize.

Up close, Jasmine thought he looked familiar. Then she gasped as she realized he had arrived on a magic flying carpet!

"We could get out of the palace," said Prince Ali, "see the world."

Jasmine looked at the carpet and hesitated.

"Do you trust me?" asked Prince Ali.

Jasmine remembered hearing those words before. "Yes," she said softly, wondering if this could be the stranger from the marketplace. Then she took his hand and stepped onto the Magic Carpet.

With a *whoosh*, the carpet took to the sky. Snuggling next to Prince Ali, Jasmine allowed a smile to spread across her face. When the two finally came to rest on a rooftop, Jasmine's suspicions were confirmed: Prince Ali actually *was* the young man she had met before.

"The truth is," he lied, "I sometimes dress as a commoner to escape the pressures of palace life."

As the thrilling night came to an end, back on the palace balcony, Jasmine said good night.

"Sleep well, Princess," Prince Ali said, before leaving her. But he could not bring himself to reveal that he was really just a poor boy named Aladdin. He had fallen for Jasmine the moment they had met, but he knew that because she was a princess, Jasmine could only marry a prince. So with the help of a magic lamp he had found and the Genie who lived in it, Aladdin had been able to transform himself into Prince Ali.

Back at the palace, Jafar was planning to marry Jasmine himself. He had discovered that Prince Ali was just a poor boy, and told Jasmine all about it. Then he stole Aladdin's magic lamp and turned himself into an all-powerful sorcerer.

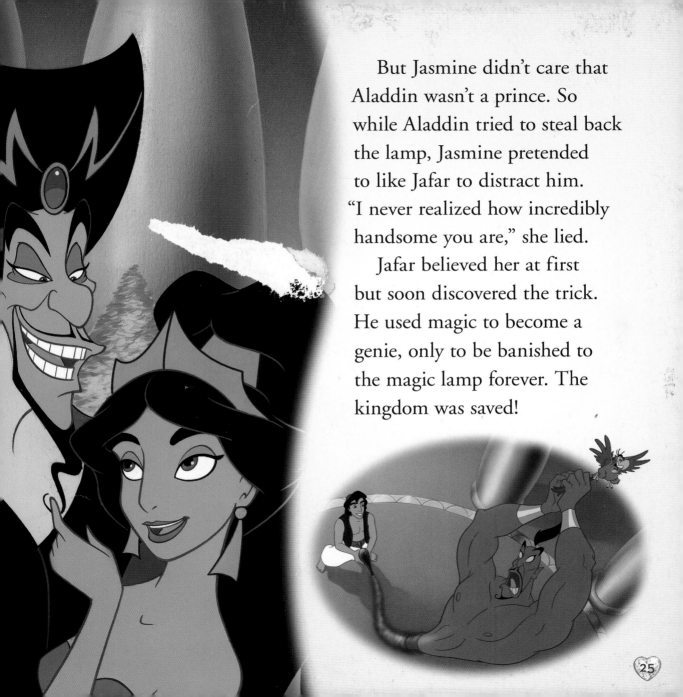

But Jasmine didn't care that Aladdin wasn't a prince. So while Aladdin tried to steal back the lamp, Jasmine pretended to like Jafar to distract him. "I never realized how incredibly handsome you are," she lied.

Jafar believed her at first but soon discovered the trick. He used magic to become a genie, only to be banished to the magic lamp forever. The kingdom was saved!

When Aladdin and Jasmine were reunited, he apologized to her for lying. "Well, I guess this is—good-bye," he said sadly.

"Oh, that stupid law!" said Jasmine. "This isn't fair. I love you!"

The Sultan realized that Aladdin had proven his worth. "From this day forth," Jasmine's father proclaimed, "the princess shall marry whomever she deems worthy."

"I choose you, Aladdin," Jasmine said with a smile. And with those words, a whole new world lay ahead of the princess and her true love.

The End

Every Disney Princess Loves to Dress Up

Dress Up

This month's princess theme is dress up.

These crafts and activities will show you different ways
to dress like a princess.

Jasmine's Crafts & Activities

There's nothing like dressing up in beautiful gowns and sparkling jewels to make you feel like a princess. Turn the page to discover Jasmine's crafts and activities all about dressing up!

Jasmine's Headband

Make a pretty headband just like Jasmine's, and wear it with princess pride!

What You Need

- Pencil
- Scissors
- Clean, empty 2-liter soda bottle
- Blue and green permanent markers
- White card stock
- Metallic gold marker
- Blue headband
- White paper
- Tape
- White glue

With a grown-up's help:

1. Trace the oval below onto white paper. Cut out the oval.

2. Tape the oval to the curved top part of the bottle as shown. Use a permanent marker to trace around the oval. Ask a grown-up to cut along the line you traced.

3. Use the blue and green markers to color the inside of the oval (the inward-curving side) so it looks just like Jasmine's jewel.

 Royal Idea

Along with her headband, Jasmine wears other pretty bands in her hair. Use blue-green bands to make a ponytail of your own. Add your special headband to complete the look.

4. Set the jewel on a piece of card stock. Carefully draw a bigger oval around the outer edge of the jewel.

5. Cut out the card stock oval. Glue the jewel to the center of the oval. Once the glue dries, carefully color the edges of the oval with the gold marker.

6. Glue the oval to the center of the headband. Once the glue dries, your new headband will be ready to wear!

Birthstone Headband

Make a personalized birthstone headband. Follow steps 2–6, using permanent markers to make the jewel in the headband look like your birthstone.

Below are all the months and their special gems:

January	February	March	April	May	June
Garnet	Amethyst	Aquamarine	Diamond	Emerald	Pearl

July	August	September	October	November	December
Ruby	Peridot	Sapphire	Pink tourmaline	Citrine	Blue topaz

31

Jasmine's Slippers

Jasmine always looks beautiful in her slippers. Make your very own slippers and add jewels and other pretty decorations for a royal look!

What You Need

- Small bowl
- 2 cups (475 ml) of water
- Food coloring (any color)
- Spoon
- Two no-longer-needed white ankle socks
- Marker
- Scissors
- White glue
- Plastic jewels, sequins, glitter glue, fabric paint, and other items to decorate your slippers

With a grown-up's help:

1. Fill a small bowl with the water. Add 10–12 drops of food coloring to the water. Stir to mix.

2. Put the socks into the water. Let them soak for about 15 minutes. Remove the socks from the water and let them dry.

3. Once the socks are dry, lay them flattened to one side. Draw half an oblong shape along the crease as shown. Cut out along the line through both layers. Repeat with the other sock.

4. Flatten out both socks so the cut parts are centered as shown.

5. Decorate your slippers with plastic jewels, sequins, glitter glue, fabric paint, or anything else you like.

6. Once the glue dries, slip your slippers onto your feet.

♡ Royal Idea

Make your slippers into musical dancing shoes. Ask a grown-up to sew a small jingle bell to each toe. You won't just be dancing to the music when you wear these shoes. You'll be making it, too!

The Color of Royalty

Standard food coloring comes in four colors: red, blue, yellow, and green. Mix them together to make other royal colors. Here are some suggestions:

- 💧 Orange = Red + Yellow
- 💧 Purple = Red + Blue
- 💧 Light green = Yellow + Green
- 💧 Brown = Red + Green

Crafts & Activities

Jasmine's Royal Finery

Jasmine loves to wear her shiny gold earrings and necklace. Borrow a little bit of Jasmine's style with golden finery of your own!

What You Need

- Heavy-duty 9-inch (23-cm)-diameter paper plate
- No-longer-needed CD or DVD
- Pencil
- Scissors
- White paper
- Paintbrush
- Gold or yellow paint
- Glitter glue
- Tape
- Two small rubber bands

With a grown-up's help:

1. Lay the paper plate facedown on a flat surface. Center the CD on the plate and trace around the outside edge of the CD.

2. Carefully draw another circle about ¾ inch (2 cm) larger around the circle you just traced. Then draw one long line and two short lines as shown.

3. Cut along all of the lines. When you are done, you will have one open-ended hoop and one CD-sized circle.

Crafts & Activities

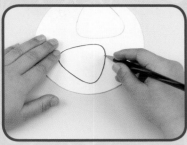

4. Trace the earring shape below onto white paper. Cut out the shape and place it on the paper plate circle. Trace around the shape in two places for two earrings.

5. Cut out the earring shapes. Then paint the uncoated side of the necklace and earrings gold or yellow. Once the paint dries, decorate the necklace and earrings with glitter glue. Let the glue dry completely. (**Hint:** Use a yellow or gold metallic paper plate if you don't want to paint your necklace and earrings.)

6. Lay the earrings facedown. Tape a rubber band to the top point of each earring as shown.

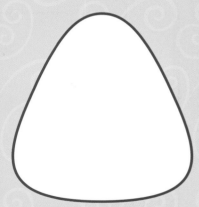

🤍 **Royal Idea**

To wear your earrings, loop the rubber bands around your ears. Adjust the earrings until you like their position. To wear your necklace, bend the loop open and place it around your neck. Slide the slits together to close your fancy neckwear.

Princess Dress Up Day

Every princess just loves getting dressed up. Treat yourself and your friends to an afternoon of dress up fun! Here is an easy way to host a princess-perfect event.

1. Tell all your friends to bring their very favorite princess clothes and accessories to your home. The more gear you gather, the more fun this activity will be.

2. Spread everything out on a bed or on the floor where everyone can see it.

3. Dress like princesses! Have fun putting together perfect outfits. It's OK to mix colors, fabric styles, and accessories. Anything goes!

4. Ask a grown-up to take pictures of you and your friends in your princess finery. These pictures will help you to remember all the fun.

5. Now it's time to do it all over again. Let everyone choose a brand-new princess outfit. Make sure everyone gets a turn wearing the clothes she likes best!

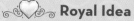 **Royal Idea**

Is there an oriental carpet or rug in your house? If so, get dressed up as Jasmine, Aladdin, or the Genie, and then ask a grown-up to take a picture of you on your "magic" carpet.

Crafts & Activities

Wouldn't it be fun to dress up like Jasmine and her friends? Here are ways to look like them.

To look like Jasmine:
Pull your hair into a ponytail. Put on some light blue, loose-flowing pants and a matching tank top. Wear the jeweled headband, necklace, earrings, and slippers you made.

To look like Aladdin:
You'll need flowing white pants, a vest, and a brown sash if you want to dress like Aladdin. Don't forget to add a little hat. Skip the shoes— Aladdin likes to go barefoot.

To look like the Genie:
Cut two wristbands from a no-longer-needed yellow sock. With a grown-up's permission, use a makeup pencil to draw a thin beard and dark eyebrows on your face. Wear a long-sleeved, blue shirt and flowing pants to create a little Genie magic!